Praise for Mario Aliberto III's
All the Dead We Have Yet to Bury

The wonderful stories in Aliberto's chapbook are haunting—literally. A wife pays for someone to be the ghost of her dead husband, a drunk man tries to follow the advice of his dead mother: again and again, the past and the present collide to dramatic and beautiful effect. Packing an emotional punch far beyond their length, these stories showcase the power of flash fiction and linger in the memory like the stories' many ghosts.

—Gwen Kirby, author of *Shit Cassandra Saw*

Aliberto III writes sentences that flare like oxygen to fire, like the burst of a firework imprinting upon the reader's eye and mind. These stories crackle and sizzle and keep the reader entertained with showing us the best of ourselves. He can flat out tell a great story, one that entertains as much as it teaches, our bodies, our hearts to keep "rising and rising and never stopping."

—Tommy Dean, author of *Hollows*

Aliberto offers a compelling catalogue of hauntings, and the writing style is sharply attuned to each unique tale. These stories crackle with energy, surprise, humor, and—most of all—a tenderness. I will be reaching for this collection again and again....

—Cheryl Pappas, author of *The Hunger of Clarity*

Masterfully waving good-bye to the spirits of those we will lose and those we have already lost, Aliberto takes us on an intimate journey through the lives of these characters as they dance along the edges of what's left.

—Melissa Llanes Brownlee, author of *Hard Skin* and *Bitter over Sweet*

All the Dead We Have Yet to Bury

Copyright © 2025 by Mario Aliberto III

Cover image and author's photo by Kylie Aliberto
Edited by Maria S. Picone
Cover design by James Rawlings and Teresa Snow

All rights reserved. No part of this publication may be reproduced, distributed or transmitted in any form or by any means, including photocopying, recording, or other electronic or mechanical methods, without the prior written permission of the publisher, except in the case of brief quotations embodied in critical reviews and certain other noncommercial uses permitted by copyright law. For permission requests, write to the publisher at the email address below.

Chestnut Review Chapbooks, an imprint of Chestnut Review LLC
Ithaca, New York

https://chestnutreview.com
ISBN: 978-1-965158-08-1

All the Dead We Have Yet to Bury

Mario Aliberto III

Chestnut Review Chapbooks

For Kylie

You. Always you.

CONTENTS

CLASSIFIED AD FOR A GHOST

I would like someone to haunt my house and simulate some of my deceased husband's habits so I can get some sleep. These include:

- Walking into the bathroom. Leaving the door open with the bathroom light shining in my face. Urinating loudly.
- Opening the refrigerator door so hard the ketchup bottle clangs the pickle jar.
- Television blaring the Yankees game in the living room and loud snoring.
- Night hauntings only. Money negotiable.
- No contact! Correspondence and payment through email and PayPal. I don't want to see you.

A week after agreeing to terms with the only respondent to her online ad, the ghost made his first appearance. Olivia lay in bed with the latest Stephen King novel, and maybe not the best choice of book, but she hoped a bit of light reading would provide some relief from insomnia. She opened the book and hissed at the blurry words on the page. The familiar urge to call out to Tully to come to bed and bring her glasses from the kitchen table had not died along with him. She stayed to her side of the bed, her body falling into the dip in the mattress, but without her husband's chest to stop her, she rolled into the valley. A sob welled in her throat when a blurry shape, a ghost if you will, entered the ensuite bathroom. The light on, the door open. A man peeing, a hard stream, not the staccato of Tully's cancerous prostate, yet it brought tears to her eyes. A toilet flush. The light clicked off. Olivia whispered thank you. She slept almost forty-five minutes straight.

A few days passed. Once again, Olivia lay in bed, this time with her glasses properly fixed over her eyes as she read a few chapters of her book by the light of the bedside lamp. She couldn't get comfortable. Fidgety, as if she were caffeinated. From the living room came the familiar sound of the television turning on. Snatches of programs as channels flipped. A crowd cheering, followed by excited commentary. Difficult to make out the words. Spanish? A sporting event, but definitely not Tully's beloved Yankees.

Goooooooaaaaaaalllllllll!

Soccer? Tully hated soccer. And yet, the Spanish announcers, the rhythm and joy in which they called the action, lulled Olivia into a tranquil space she hadn't known existed. A space outside her grief. The ghost made the odd snoring noise, obviously fake, and intentionally or not, ridiculously over the top. Olivia giggled. Was that the ghost laughing as well? She put her book down and removed her glasses. She turned the bedside lamp off. An hour of uninterrupted sleep until she awoke in silence. Unable to quell her curiosity, she searched the house but found everything as she left it. As if her visitor were really a ghost.

Weeks passed, and the hauntings occurred more frequently. Olivia always in bed. When the ghost made itself known, she would take her glasses off if she hadn't already. Blurry glimpses as the ghost moved about the house, Tully on her mind. She'd listen to the sound of the refrigerator door opening, the condiments shifting on shelves, their satisfying clink. The microwave door opening and the beeping timer. The smell of food, a spicy aroma the house had never known in the time prior to Tully's passing. Sleep would take her gently. The noise of the television still on sometimes after she woke from an hour or two of rest. No longer soccer, but movies, Spanish musicals with incredible scores. The instruments swept her along, and the ballads, while she could not understand the words, she understood their meaning. Occasionally, the ghost sang along, his voice high, a little pitchy, but tender.

"Si tengo que volver a amar, elijo amar solo a tu fantasma."

The ghost visited every night—the bathroom, the peeing, the singing—and every morning left no trace. Until one night she heard him cracking and stirring eggs. The smell of onions and peppers. Frying bacon. She tiptoed into the kitchen, and although there was no sign of the ghost, she discovered a covered dish and a yellow Post-It note on the counter. Beautiful looping cursive. *Please eat something.* Beneath the cover, a flour tortilla stuffed with green and red peppers, onions, scrambled eggs. Crispy bits of bacon. She hadn't been eating, but now she was ravenous. With a full stomach, Olivia slept three hours, waking when she rolled into the bed's valley expecting Tully's chest to hold her up, only to be reminded he was gone.

That night, she kept her glasses on when she went to bed. Only her bedside lamp issued light. She wanted to see the ghost. It didn't matter what he looked like, but she could no longer imagine him as Tully. She listened to the creaks and groans of the house settling. She waited. The taste of the breakfast burrito lingered on her tongue. She read her book until it became obvious the ghost would not be making an appearance. Disappointed, she turned off the lamp and placed her glasses atop her book. She rolled back and something prevented her from continuing into the mattress's dip. The warmth of a chest pressed to her back. Knees tucked into the backs of her knees, legs filling the shape her legs left. Breath on her neck. A hand reached for hers, fingers trembling. She closed her eyes. She slept the night through.

THE SWEAR JAR

The girl in the pool was perfectly safe.

Greg knew that.

From behind the snack counter at Spring Hill Public Pool, Greg used his apron to fan away the apparition of meatsmoke wafting from the grill. The Saturday pre-lunch crowd lounged around the water as children splashed about, the sun shining generously upon shoulders pink as raw burger patties. He watched the blonde girl wearing arm floaties toddle around the shallow end. She had to be about two, maybe three. Same age as his baby sister, Grace.

blue sky   barbecue   aunt and uncle coming over   plastic kiddie pool in the shape of a turtle in the backyard   they use the pool for the dog   he fills the pool with water from the garden hose   little Grace loves the pool   she loves strawberries and Sesame Street and him   she   loves   him

He found an area on his apron not stained with grease and mopped sweat from his eyes. The tiny girl began to shimmy along the side of the pool away from the shallow end. Two lifeguards from Greg's high school who were a grade above him sat beneath the umbrella shade of their opposing lifeguard chairs with noses buried in phones.

Where were her parents?

The snack counter manager, DeAnna, finished ringing up a Gatorade and Skittles for a dripping wet boy holding onto the waistband of his oversized board shorts with a death grip. Greg liked working for her. A stoner college dropout whose idea of managing consisted of freezing burgers and hot dogs left over at the end of shift to be reheated the next day, she never gave him any trouble. When there were no customers, she hid in the back puffing on her vape, occasionally offering him a hit.

The blonde girl clung desperately to the side of the pool. What if Greg was the only one watching her? He pointed at the girl in the pool with his spatula. "Fucking lifeguards need to get off their phones."

"How about you worry about the burgers." DeAnna picked up the plastic gallon jug with a blue lid near the grill and shook it. A few coins rattled. In its former life, the jug had been an economy-sized mayonnaise container, but the label had been scraped off and replaced with a taped-on yellow paper proclaiming it The Mother F'n Swear Jar. "Pay up."

"Seriously?"

DeAnna playfully shook the jar in Greg's face. "F-bomb costs two bucks."

Greg flipped a couple of burgers, removed a few that looked done, and set his spatula aside. He took out his wallet and sorted a twenty, a five, and a couple of singles. DeAnna presented the jar, and he dropped the singles inside. She thanked him for his "charitable donation," lifting the jar overhead and singing a high-pitched note as if the swear jar were something to be exalted. He suspected she spent the money on her vape. He didn't mind. At least she shared. At the counter, a mother with green eyeshadow and salon-styled hair coughed, and four boys pawed through the candy rack. DeAnna took their order. Greg searched the pool for the girl.

blue sky   barbecue   parents inside with his aunt and uncle watching the Florida game   Grace splashing in the pool   the dog barking and chasing a squirrel   the dog hops the fence and he has to get the dog out of the street before a car comes   he tells Grace not to move   why does he tell her not to move

Greg stood on his toes to look over the head of the lady at the counter. A pair of arm floaties bobbed in the water like dead fish.

blue sky   barbecue   he saves the dog   the damn dog

He put his palms flat on the counter to boost himself up. The mother stepped back and pinched her sundress closed over her bikini top. "Move," he said. He vaulted the counter, caught the candy rack with his foot, and sent bags of Skittles flying. The boys gathered candy to their sticky, wet chests as he ran past.

Greg pushed through the crowd. He started with the deep end. Nothing but splashing and squealing kids. He balanced precariously on the pool's edge, scanning the water. He stripped his apron and threw it behind him.

"Grace…" He bent his knees to leap when he saw the little girl's blonde hair—

blue sky   barbecue   blonde hair fans out in the pool water like a plucked sunflower

—and her mother holding her afloat and telling her to use "big scoops" with her hands and kick her legs.

People gave him space. His face wet. Breathing but no air. Their whispers might as well have been shouts. His sister. So young. The poor baby. How deep? Oh my God. That's horrible. Last year. His sister. So young. A few inches of water. Terrible. His sister. Have to watch them. His sister.

The little blonde girl was safe. Someone watched after her. Three years old at the most. The age Grace was. No. The age Grace would always be.

DeAnna appeared next to him, took him by the shoulders, and pulled him away from the pool. She walked him behind the snack counter. The burgers were burned. He couldn't find his apron to wipe his face.

"You need to find a new job, dude. You can't keep doing this to yourself." DeAnna offered him her vape. "What if I wasn't here to save you?"

Greg ignored the vape and picked up the swear jar. He twisted the lid off, letting it skitter on the counter. He removed the twenty and the five from his wallet. He stuffed the money inside the jar and then pressed his face to the jar's opening. A curse ripped from his throat, without a beginning, without an end.

FROGGER

Night in Tampa is never dark, no never, cigar bar neon signs, nightclub strobe lights, traffic signals on wires swaggering to the drums of Cuban street music, the rumble of car engines, and I'm swigging from a bottle of Tito's in a brown bag, and why do I never buy enough Coke for a mixer, easily remedied, a bodega across the street, once all the cars pass, and if my mother were here, if my mother were still alive, she wouldn't like me standing this close to the street, this is the city after all, and all these cars, she was right, they really do not give a fuck about me, and jeez, they drive fast, and the little crosswalk man is lit up red, and I'm waiting for the red crosswalk man to turn to white, the way my mother taught me when I was a little boy, held my hand from one side of the street to the other, and away from her I've never been good at heeding warning signs, not as an adult, not without her, and I know I could get across one lane, maybe two, time it right and I could possibly totally Frogger it to the other side, well, no, probably not, but what if I could, what if this is my calling, the one thing in life I'm finally good at, my purpose, and if I don't try I'll never know, I mean, I have to be good at something, because I've never been good at anything, not little league, or culinary school, or sobriety, or making amends to my mother even though my sister begged me to come to the hospital before it was too late, and if my mother were here, if she were still alive, she'd say everyone has something special about them, and yeah, this could be my thing, to hop, hop, hop safely to the other side, and this stranger next to me is watching me, like he could catch me before I leap lily pad to lily pad, and I don't want to be squashed but I want to know if there's anything special about me, if my mother was right to believe in me, the same way she believed I'd pay her back all the money I borrowed, hold on to a job, get sober, and I take a deep breath, load my legs to spring, and as the wind of a car whips by, the man next to me gasps, and this is it, I can do this, and I leap, but not before the little cross walk man changes from red to white, tiny white dots, tiny constellation of a walking man, and all the cars stop like time itself is frozen, it's safe to cross now, the white cross walk man says so, the man next to me leading the way says so, and if my mother were here, if my mother were still alive, she would say so, and as I watch the herd of people cross, I sip my Tito's, think about buying a Coke, all the while whispering under my breath, *Nothin special about me Momma, nothin special about me at all.*

THE LEGEND OF PANERA PARIAH

Before there were no more every-other-weekends at her father's apartment, before she remembered it as the last time he brushed her hair off her face and kissed her goodnight, Kaley begged her father for a few more stories about growing up in Plant City with his infamous cousin, Panera Pariah.

Panera Pariah, her father said on one of their Saturday nights together, his hands stinking of gasoline and lawn clippings as he tucked her into bed, *flapped her arms and flew from Plant City to Ybor City alongside a flock of Snowy Egrets because no one ever bothered to tell her a little girl couldn't fly.*

Honestly, Kaley never considered her parents divorced. Ten years old now, alternating weekends with her parents had become a seamless routine, and it wasn't like her parents hated each other. Kaley's father promised he'd come home when he got right. Said he was halfway there. Kaley held onto the belief he'd make it all the way home someday. As for Kaley's mother, she still wore her wedding ring. In fact, her mother always said Kaley's father was the love of her life, but sometimes love wasn't enough to keep people together.

Kaley believed they'd be a family again right up to the Monday her mother got that phone call. No one had ever cried as hard as her mother when she broke the news to Kaley, barely able to get the words out. Kaley's father had been at work, mowing grass for the Plant City lawn crew, when on a forty-five-degree incline along an embankment of a city culvert, his riding mower flipped, pinning him beneath a foot of water. Her mother said it was quick. No pain. In the coming days, an online news article would quote a witness claiming her father drowned before the mower blades stopped spinning.

Panera Pariah, her father had said, breath beer-sweet, eyes glassy-red, *wore white to funerals and black to weddings because she knew there was a little sweet and a little sad in everything.*

In the school auditorium, Ms. Franklin discussed all the changes a girl's body experienced during puberty. Ms. Franklin played a video on the big screen for the sixth-grade girls, and they learned all about hair growing in their armpits and on their privates, breast development and menstruation. Hormones and reproduction. Ms. Franklin taught them everything about when life began, but nothing about when life ended.

Sitting in her bedroom after picking up her things from her father's apartment, Kaley wondered about all the important stuff Ms. Franklin had left out. What did you do with the duffel bag you no longer needed to pack on Thursday nights? Where did you put the extra hairbrush and toothbrush and sets of underwear? The extra pajamas, board games, and nail polish. The second night light. The second mattress. The second Nintendo. The second television. What did you do if you had two of everything except two parents?

Panera Pariah, her father had told her, his eyes glittering in the bedroom nightlight, *ate soup with chopsticks and never spilled a drop.*

The day of her father's celebration of life, Kaley picked a white dress to wear, and her mother, instead of fussing over the color, wore white as well. At the funeral home, Kaley kept an eye on the door, waiting for her father's cousin to make a grand entrance. On a pedestal at the front of the room, water lilies and chrysanthemums surrounded her father's urns. His ashes had been divided between a large silver urn and a smaller urn about the size of a teacup. The large one for Kaley, the small one for her grandmother.

Panera Pariah, her father had whispered before brushing her hair aside and placing a last kiss upon her cheek, *could step through a mirror and play with her reflection. She said that way she was never alone and always had copies of her favorite things.*

Mourners waited in line to hug Kaley's mother as if she were a widow. They hugged her grandmother and patted the uncles on the back. Everyone in black. No sign of her father's cousin. People settled in their seats, and one of her uncles stood by her father's urns to speak, but when he began sobbing and couldn't get a word out, Kaley's mother rushed to his side and told stories. Some Kaley knew, some she didn't. Everyone laughed. Everyone cried. It was good in the worst way.

After the service, Kaley and her mother were the last ones left besides her Grandma. Kaley held the large urn, her Grandma the small one. The door to the funeral home opened, and Kaley held her breath with anticipation for Panera Pariah's arrival. Unfortunately, it was only the funeral director ushering them out so he could prepare the room for the next service. As they hugged goodbye, Kaley's mother eyed the small urn in Grandma's hands. She twisted her wedding ring, her hands empty.

Kaley stopped her Grandma at the door. "He's supposed to come home with us. He promised." Grandma shook her head. Looked at the wedding ring on Kaley's mother's finger. Then the wedding ring on her own finger. Six years since Grandpa passed and her hand never went without it. "Not halfway," Kaley said. "All the way."

That night, Kaley's mother tucked Kaley into bed beside two urns on the nightstand. She rested her head on Kaley's lap, crying with all the hurt in the world. "You brought him home."

Kaley brushed the hair off her mother's face and kissed her cheek. She whispered in her mother's ear, "Panera Pariah wears white to funerals, owns two of everything, and her love is enough to keep everyone together."

ALL APOLOGIES

Margarite tuned her acoustic guitar, contemplating a song to play for her AP English students, when the ghost entered the classroom. The ghost wore a light green bed sheet, two jagged holes cut out for piercing blue eyes. The sheet's hem, a filthy brown ring as if the ghost had dragged it through puddles, scraped the tops of black and white All-Star Converse sneakers. On the white toe of the left Converse, the word CORPO-RATE was written in black Sharpie, and on the right, SELL-OUT. Sneakers and handwriting Margarite recognized as Kurt Cobain's.

Margarite cleared her throat, anxious to dive back into the semester's poetry section. The students, a mix of baggy t-shirts and skater shorts, loose sweaters and ripped jeans, shifted uncomfortably at their desks as Kurt took a seat in the front row. Sensing the tension around Kurt's presence, Margarite strummed the opening chords to "Smells Like Teen Spirit." Margarite believed teens were more responsive to poetry when introduced through music, and she could think of no better choice than Nirvana. Kurt's songs had meant so much to her when she was their age.

Then, Margarite growled the song's haunting first line. Kurt tapped a Converse. In the back of the room, goth cheerleaders in black uniforms and black lipstick shook pompoms through lethargic choreography. She hadn't even seen them enter the classroom. The rest of the students stood and began bouncing on their heels in a desultory mosh pit. It was just like the music video for "Smells Like Teen Spirit", except where the video was one of teenage angst and rebellion, Margarite could only describe the scene before her as utter despair.

Margarite allowed the last guitar not to trail off. Students returned to their desks and bowed their heads. She didn't want her kids to be sad. The way she was the day after Kurt took his life, watching "Smells Like Teen Spirit" on loop. She had believed the poetry of his music could help her kids make sense of their feelings, the way Kurt's music comforted her after he went away. Maybe knowing she went through the same thing would help them. She looked at Kurt, recalled how his death made her feel. She ditched the guitar and scribbled out a prose poem on a piece of paper, the words flowing along with her tears. When she was finished, she read it aloud to her students while staring into Kurt's eyes.

Dear Kurt,

There's a moment during Nirvana's MTV Unplugged Session captured on a poster in my bedroom, camera tight on you, green sweater open over a white tee, cigarette smoldering between the fingers of your right hand, acoustic guitar balanced on your lap like a child, your pool-water blue eyes cast to the sky, lips slightly parted, like someone fragile discovering faith, and yet, if asked, I'd say you look perfectly content, and I'd say how sad it makes me you couldn't make it last, because like all good things, a good song, a good life, a good world, maybe you thought, how could it get better than this, and now I see it was not contentment, but surrender, and I wish I could have convinced you to hold on, but I already know what you'd have said: nevermind.

—Margarite

Kurt raised his hand which looked like a formless growth beneath his sheet. The students shivered as if a cold wind passed through them. Kurt patted his desk. Margarite was

confused at first, then placed her poem on his desk. Kurt
tapped the poem with a sheeted finger. *How did she feel today*
he seemed to want to know. She picked up a pen and lined out
words. Once again, she read aloud.

Dear Kurt,
~~There's~~ <u>*a moment*</u> ~~during Nirvana's MTV Unplugged Ses-~~
~~sion captured on a poster in my bedroom, camera~~ <u>*is*</u> ~~tight on~~
~~you, green sweater open over a white tee, cigarette smoldering~~
~~between the fingers of your right hand, acoustic guitar bal-~~
~~anced on your lap~~ <u>*like a child,*</u> ~~your pool-water blue eyes cast~~
~~to the sky, lips slightly parted, like someone~~ <u>*fragile*</u> ~~discover-~~
~~ing faith,~~ <u>*and yet, if*</u> ~~asked, I'd say~~ <u>*you*</u> ~~look perfectly con-~~
~~tent, and I'd say how sad it makes me you~~ <u>*couldn't make it,*</u>
~~last, because like all good things, a good song, a good life, a~~
~~good world, maybe you thought,~~ <u>*how could*</u> ~~it get better than~~
~~this, and now~~ <u>*I*</u> ~~see it was~~ <u>*not*</u> ~~contentment, but~~ <u>*surrender?*</u>
~~and I wish I could have convinced you to hold on, but I already~~
~~know what you'd have said: nevermind.~~
—Margarite

When Margarite looked up from her reading, all the students were crying. Beside her, she was surprised to find the
janitor from the music video, an old man in blue coveralls,
swaying side to side holding onto a mop like a metronome.
The words GRIEF COUNSELING written in chalk on the
blackboard behind him. Kurt waved his ghostly arms beneath
the sheet as if conducting an orchestra, encouraging the students to write their feelings as Margarite had.

The students wrote. Their words: sad, depression, anxiety,
sad, no hope, no hope at all, sad, sad, sad all the time, why,
why'd she do it, why'd she leave us, why didn't she love us
enough to stay?

Oh, the poor dears! She should play them a song.

Margarite tuned her acoustic guitar, contemplating a song to play for her AP English students, when the ghost exited the classroom. She decided on "All Apologies." She attempted to strum the strings, but a bed sheet draped over her body blocked her fingers, and she could no longer remember the words.

SHOOTING AT HURRICANES

Jackson sat on the flat roof of Pop-Pop's single-story condo overlooking Clearwater Beach with a rifle laid across his legs. Wind gusts pushed thirty-miles-an-hour, and waves taller than a grown man broke upon the shore. He should have checked the weather before he caught a flight on a C17 from Kandahar a couple of days ago, but he was Florida born and raised and he wasn't scared of hurricane season. No storm could've have stopped him.

Earlier, The Weather Channel served as background noise as he searched the condo for something Pop-Pop would want him to have. Something with meaning. Only things worth a shit were the old man's military medals and Remington .223 rifle. Didn't feel right taking medals another man earned. But the rifle was the same one he and Pop-Pop breathed on when he was a boy learning to shoot on the beer can range behind their old ranch home in Plant City, before Pop-Pop retired to Clearwater Beach

The Weather Channel kept talking about a bunch of crazy people with guns bragging about shooting up the hurricane. Before the background of a trailer park, a reporter interviewed shirtless men in jean shorts, women in American flag bikini tops. Everyone obviously drunk and "trailer trash" written all over the reporter's face. The banner on the bottom of the news report constantly reminded people, seriously, do not shoot at the hurricane.

Now, sitting on the roof, waiting for the storm, the rifle rested on Jackson's lap like a pet that could find no more comfortable place in all the world. Gun oil reek from cleaning. One in the chamber, *Semper Fi mother fucker, hoorah!* Down in the Gulf, he watched a lone surfer on a red surfboard get dumped every time the surfer attempted to paddle out past the break. The horizon erased between the grey water and the black reckoning of sky. Wind gust strong enough if he opened his mouth his cheeks flapped like a hound dog's hanging out a car window. Rain was still offshore but would arrive soon enough.

He couldn't believe Pop-Pop went in so ordinary a way. Man was a war hero by God. Purple heart. Silver star. Hospital must have got his name and number from Pop-Pop's emergency contacts after the heart attack. Nothing to do but wait for the storm to pass and see about arranging the military sendoff the old man earned.

The surfer wiped out again.

Since he was the one that got the call, it meant Pa and Pop-Pop never made up. Hell, he'd barely talked to Pa himself. Phone calls only, hadn't seen him. Chatting about nothing but the weather ever since he signed up for the Marines the day after graduation and Pa called him a damn fool and cursed Pop-Pop for putting such an idiotic idea into his head with all the war stories. The fight to end all fights the night before he left for boot camp. Pa pleaded with him not to be a soldier. Go to college or get a job. Hell, be a mechanic like him. Pa said wasn't a government in all the world worth killing yourself or others for. Said the Marines valued his life same as a gun values a bullet.

Pop-Pop had fought in Vietnam and Pa always said Pop-Pop might have been better off as to have died over there then come back the way he did.

Well. That was something.

He didn't understand it then. He understood it now.

The Gulf of Mexico had become a grey washing machine,

and he spotted the red surfboard a solid minute before he caught sight of the surfer clinging to it. Too far away for him to help. The surfer was in it and would have to get himself out. He ran his hand back and forth along the rifle stock, clearing away grains of sand. A clean gun was a happy gun. Sir, yes sir.

Jackson had spent his last four years in the Marines and most of them on foreign sand. He had some leave to take when he got the call about Pop-Pop. His CO was sweet on him reenlisting and granted his request. He'd liked to have asked Pop-Pop what he should do if he decided he had enough. Pop-Pop never talked about how the person you are when you ship off isn't the person you are when you ship back. How a war story is only a story if it didn't happen to you.

The surfer got himself to the beach and collapsed, red board pooled beneath him, resting beyond the reach of the waves, beyond the reach of everything it seemed. The surfer reminded him of a few buddies left over in the shit covered in sand and blood.

He didn't like to think of those boys much.

He thought of those boys all the time.

He fit Pop-Pop's rifle stock to his shoulder, leveled the gun, and looked down the iron sights. The storm was still offshore. But it was coming. He closed one eye. Zeroed in on the storm's black heart.

He could have been a mechanic like Pa said, but this is who he was.

He clicked the safety off.

Finger on the trigger.

Bang.

He imagined the bullet caught up in the hurricane, circling and circling. Might even come back on him. He figured that might be the truth of it. Was he anything more than a bullet

Pop-Pop fired circling back to hit Pa's heart?

He wanted to pick up the phone. Tell Pa he was sorry. Scream he needed help the way he was screaming it in his head. But he wasn't going to do none of that.

He put the rifle down and stood and spread his arms. Made himself an easy target. He closed his eyes. He waited. Wind was hot. Crap flying everywhere. Sand in his teeth. Might as well have been back in the shit over there. He was always in the shit.

This. This is what Pop-Pop left him.

Pa had warned him. Goddamn it. Goddamn it.

IMPACT

In another timeline, I'm not a wife screaming about your obsession with planes, your obsession with flying away from us, and an egret isn't caught in the propeller of your Cessna, isn't fanned into bloody feathers stuccoing the plane's windshield, and the engine hasn't quit, and your final radio transmission isn't you shouting you're going to glide this one out, zero visibility, Brace, Brace, Brace....

In another timeline, a storm comes through, and you push your takeoff time back, or better yet, cancel the trip entirely, schedule the flight for another day, choosing to spend time with me, with your kids, instead of once again flying off into the clouds, and the egret finds a place to stay dry and dreams of delicious worms after the rain passes.

In another timeline, we take the kids bicycling over steaming asphalt in a V formation like we are a flock of egrets, and you talk about how wrong it feels to not to be in the air, how you hate being grounded, and I remind you that you can let go of the handlebars, put your arms out to your side, let the bike coast and look up at the sky, and is this not flying?

But in this timeline, the kids and I ride bikes to the beach without you, and I let go of the handlebars, arms out to the side....

I am left gliding
Zero visibility
Shouting Brace, Brace, Brace

CLOSER THAN GONE

On nights like tonight, when the ghost was foremost on Brady Scrugg's mind, he abandoned his Tampa apartment for the dive bar on the corner. Better to be flush with whiskey, surrounded by people, than endure a haunting sober and alone. It wasn't a sports pub, but there was always a Rays game on the solitary television above the bar. By Brady's fifth Old Fashioned he was nearly there, thoughts muddled like the fruit at the bottom of his whiskey glass. The ghost was close to gone, only a tiny, lingering specter at the edge of his thoughts.

And yet.

Brady picked up on a sound, verging on imperceptible, beneath the clamor of drunken debate. Something beneath the incoherent arguments of the wasted men seated next to him. The sound intermittent, like the drips of a leaky faucet. He finally traced its origin to the television over the assembly of liquor bottles, the men's faces turned up to the glow of a baseball game. Marlins in town playing the Rays.

Thok.

The contact of bat on ball. It reminded him. It reminded him.

He saw a ghost once.

A lifetime ago, ten, maybe eleven years old, out in front of the second-floor condominium his mother rented when they lived in Miami, during the engorged heat of a summer without rain. Every day Brady's mother dragged him from the kitchen window overlooking the street, slapped his Rays cap on his head, and pushed him out the door to join the pack of fatherless boys…

…stick arms and tank tops,
jean shorts and skinny legs,
fruit punch-stained lips,
peachfuzz faces premonitions of impending manhood.

Daylong games of stoopball. The thok of the rubber handball as it bounced off the steps and the scrabble of sneakers as they chased it into the street. Wrestling and throwing each other down over possession of a ball the size and color of a plum. The fatherless boys' view of masculinity inherited from the rough men that passed in and out of their mothers' lives. Brady's own mother hadn't allowed a man in their lives since his father left.

It was Brady's turn to throw. The hot butter smell of scorched asphalt. The boys expected nothing, and he usually delivered. Hard punches to his shoulders disguised as greetings. They snatched the Rays cap from his head in an impromptu rally of keep away. Their limp-wristed mocking and exaggerated lisps as they taunted him.

Growing bored because Brady offered them no challenge, they tossed him his cap. Then, one of the boys threw a fastball at Brady's chest. The rubber ball hit him square, his hands clapping together empty in that spastic way of a boy who had never played catch with a father. He scrambled after the ball as it rolled into the street. He rubbed his chest where surely a bruise would develop. The other boys laughed.

Brady didn't know self-hatred back then, only heat that prickled beneath his skin, a simmering below the surface that he tamped down, down, down, into the blackest pit of his stomach.

The boys whined for Brady to get on with it. He spun his cap backwards, performed his customary skip to get started, and ran at the stoop. He sidearmed the ball, skipping it off *the* sidewalk just beneath the bottom step. It rebounded off the stoop high into the air. He felt it as soon as he let it go. He had played the angle perfectly, and if the ball hit off the building across the street on a fly, it would be a home run. He turned around to point his finger and talk shit, but instead he saw the ghost.

A man in an ill-fitting cream-colored suit. Tie askew and stubbled cheeks.

The ghost had the dull-eyed gaze of a man listening to music only he could hear. He smelled sour, like a glass of Brady's mother's wine gone to spoil. The ghost wiped sweat from his brow with the sleeve of his jacket, his form superimposed over the background of boys chasing the ball like a pack of dogs.

Then, as if only just taking notice of Brady, the ghost's face grew serious. "What are you doing here?" A fleeting glance towards the apartment window on the second floor. A dim recognition flashed over his features. He brushed saliva from his lips with his knuckles. Eyes red and rheumy. "That's funny. I see. My mistake." Keys jingled in his hand, the sound of which seemed to startle him. He looked around, squinted into the sun, then looked back at Brady. "You got big, kid."

Brady had no words, only an urge to run to his mother.

The ghost looked up at the second-floor window once more. He shook his keys and pointed at Brady's apartment. "Is your mother…?" The ghost nodded his head, as if he'd answered his own question. Snorted. Wiped his nose. The ghost tapped the brim of the boy's cap. "Rays fan, huh? I'm a Marlins guy."

Then the other boys returned, screaming and tussling over the ball, arguing over who was next up to bat. They went silent when they saw the ghost, gaping with crooked jaws, malicious glints in their eyes. They formed a circle around Brady.

"Who are you, man?"

"Yeah, beat it, dude."

"You some pervert or something? Fuck outta here."

"Okay, boys." The ghost twirled the key ring on his finger, the jingling like glass breaking. He stumbled down the sidewalk, and over his shoulder said, "Hell of an arm you got there, kid. See you around."

Nothing to stop Brady's lower lip from quivering. The surreal quality of the world felt flimsy, the substance of notebook loose-leaf. If he reached out before him, he might touch the street, the cars, the sky, the world entire, and discover they were only a child's drawing, crumpling like a paper ball in his hands.

The other boys stood guard until they could no longer see the ghost. They patted Brady on the back. Told him how good his home run was. The best one they'd seen. They pretended not to see the tears welling. The game continued. He only lasted another inning before he quit, way before the streetlights came on.

Brady retreated to his mother's kitchen and poured a glass of cold milk. Not because he was thirsty, but only to hold something. The milk grew warm. He was afraid to drink it. Afraid it would pour right through him. Outside, he heard the boys—

Thok.

Cheers raised up from the street.

A rock in his throat he could not swallow. Vision watery.

"What are you doing?" His mother entered the kitchen and spun him around. "Are you crying?"

How to explain it? Her hands upon him, however, he could not feel her touch, as if he himself might be a ghost.

Thok.

Shouts from the boys down below. Different, as if he had

never truly heard them before. Cheers that were not cheers, but cries, wails of loneliness and wanting. Howling of the damned from their place in Hell.

"I saw him," he sobbed.

She ran to the window, swept the curtain aside. She stood very still for a very long time. "He's a drunk. He forgets he doesn't live here. You don't worry about him. He's never given us a dime. He's dead to us. Remember?"

Brady took his Rays cap off and dropped it on the floor.

His mother picked his cap up and placed it on the counter. "Dead. Understand?"

He nodded, yes, but no. No, he did not.

She pressed him to her chest and kissed the top of his head and said all the things that mothers say when there are no fathers. Brady came back to himself, but only a little. Breath in and out, eyes blinking, but not there, not really.

Haunting his own body.

The roar of the men in the dingy bar startled him back to the present. To the game on television. A fresh glass of whiskey Brady didn't recall ordering. The rowdy men screamed at the batter, pounding the bar with their fists. Brady knocked the bottom of his glass to the bar, tried to match their rhythm.

Thok.

A home run. Game over. Rays win. The men exploded in rapture, high-fiving and hugging. Pushed and shoved one another. Brady raised his whiskey in salute. One of the drunks stumbled and knocked into Brady's arm, spilling his drink.

An apology. A hard slap on his back. He felt that.

The men paid their tab and stepped out of the bar, whooping into the night.

Brady followed, whiskey glass in hand. He stared at the line of brick buildings, the passing traffic, and beneath the thrumming heartbeat of the city, if he listened closely, he could hear those boys playing stoopball still. He looked at the whiskey glass. At the building across the street. He reared back and threw the glass with everything he had.

Thok.

A home run. A hell of an arm.

The men stopped and cheered. Brady tilted his chin to the stars and joined his voice to the howls of fatherless boys rising and rising and never stopping.

TUESDAY MAY NEVER COME

The Price is Right is on television in the media room again, and no matter how many times Bernie's seen it, he can't guess the price of a can of Hunt's tomato sauce to save his life, which Laura teases him about every time he gets it wrong, and she guards the remote on her wheelchair's armrest where he can't reach it from the couch, hasn't been able to reach it in the three months since his kids sold his house and abandoned him at Suncoast Senior Living, where Laura is always first to the media room and the remote, and he wants to complain about how unfair it all is to Patty, his wife of fifty-something years, who knew the exact dates of the kids' birthdays, the anniversaries, all the grandkids' names and ages, just like she would have known he doesn't want to watch *The Price is Right* because *Law & Order* reruns are playing on another channel, the original *L & O*, none of those spin-offs which he hates, and Patty would know what day it was, because all Bernie knows is it isn't Tuesday, because if today were Tuesday, Laura would be wheeled off to bingo with her clucking girlfriends, and he'd have the remote on the couch next to him, and he could play detective for a little while, solve cases with Detective Briscoe, the grizzled vet who doesn't have time for anyone slowing him down as he hunts murderers and brings them to justice, and Bernie wonders who Detective Briscoe is partnered with this episode, he's had a few partners over the years, and on Tuesdays that's how it is for Bernie, he's the new partner, and Det. Briscoe assesses him, wondering if he's up to snuff, if he has what it takes, what horrors he's seen, and Bernie could tell him about his thirty years on the road as a cor-

porate accounts manager for a national coffee chain, and true
horror is all the time he spent away from his family, and when
he thinks back on the years the images cycle through many
things he wishes he could forget, peeking over the curtains
during Patty's three C-sections, watching the doctors pull the
babies past her intestines, wondering if she'd ever be put back
right, or Patty's voice on the phone calls to him on the road,
the phone call when their oldest boy cut his wrist in their bathroom, or the phone call the first time their baby girl returned
home with a purple bruise on her cheek and claimed she fell,
or the phone call about how their middle-child moved out in
the middle of the night without saying goodbye, or how after
fifty-something years he rose out of bed one morning and Patty
didn't, though they agreed when it was time for them to go he
should go first, how after all those years of being a husband,
a father, he didn't know how to be either, and all those retire-
ment years of watching *Law & Order* reruns he didn't have
the first clue what to do when he couldn't wake his dear, sweet
Patty, didn't know which of his kids to call or if they would
answer, didn't know how to tell them, didn't know how to talk
to them, had never really talked to them, and what does he
have to say other than he's sorry, it should be him, but before
he can tell Det. Briscoe any of that and settle the question of
his fitness for duty, they're grabbing their suit coats and rush-
ing out of the precinct, because there's always another body
on Tuesday, another case to solve, and he knows to stay close
because Det. Briscoe knows exactly what to do, who to call,
what comes next, he's a great partner, and Bernie hasn't had a
new partner for fifty-plus years, and yes, he could ask Laura to
change the channel, could tell her all about Tuesdays and the
cases he investigates while she's stamping green ink on num-

bered squares, how life is unfair, how little people value it and how quickly it can be taken away, how one day will be the last day he watches *Law & Order*, and he'll be under a sheet and his life will remain a mystery he was never able to solve, and Bernie turns to Laura, and her head slowly creaks in his direction, and she's squinting at him, hand on the remote, studying him as if he's a prize on the Showcase Showdown she's never seen before, while he wonders if she's up to snuff, if she has what it takes, what horrors she's seen.

GOODBYE, TAMPA

Feigning sleep in the passenger seat of her father's pick-up truck, Cammy listened to the tap, tap, tap of his wedding ring on the steering wheel bid her adieu. The bon voyage sound of tires sluicing over the glittering asphalt of I-4. The world reeled by in frames. A shredded tire like the back of a black alligator in the road. Cars casting off food wrappers in their wake like brides fleeing the altar shedding their veils. The contents of her bedroom tied down in the truck bed and an acceptance letter from Florida State University saved in her phone.

"You okay? Want to hit a drive-thru?" Her father's voice surprised her, its gritty timbre compounded by his morning cigarette.

Cammy rolled her window down to counter the nicotine stink blowing in her face. The wind whipped her hair across her eyes. "Not hungry."

Supposedly, her father had quit smoking before she was born, only recently taking it up again after her mother passed. He was up to a pack a day. The cigarette piped between his lips beneath his thick mustache. When she was younger, she used to beg her father to stop being weird and grow a beard. None of Cammy's friends' fathers had mustaches. Twenty-five years in the fire department, and aside from the mustache, he'd always been clean shaven, claiming a beard would prevent him from forming a good seal on his oxygen mask inside a burning building. Cammy's mother used to claim a beard could kill him. All those nights worrying he wouldn't make it home, until his goodnight kiss would wake her, his smooth cheeks touching hers, the tickle of his mustache on her cheek.

Funny, how she was always so worried about losing him to a fire, she never once envisioned her life without her mother.

Cammy kicked her feet onto the dash and rubbed her bare legs in a way that felt like a luxury. Smooth. She had shaved them just that morning. Her grief counselor taught her feeling good on the outside could lead to feeling good on the inside. And her counselor was right. She felt better. Pieces at a time.

"Promise me you'll Facetime me," Cammy said. "Every day."

"I hate Facetime." A jowl like a fleshy hammock beneath his chin jiggled as he spoke. How big would it grow? Big like the black circles around his eyes.

"Whatever. Just call me. Promise?"

"Sure, kid. I promise." Her father grinded his cigarette in the ashtray like a responsible fireman. Eyes wet and voice cracking, smoke leaking out of his mouth, he said, "I probably don't have to say it, but I feel like I should. Your mom would be really proud of you. You know that, right?"

Cammy leaned over and kissed his cheek, stubble bristling against her lips, rough and coarse, tiny little knives cutting her to pieces. It seemed to her, life was little more than a succession of farewells. Goodbye high school. Goodbye home-cooked meals. Goodbye weekends at the mall.

"You good, kid?" Her father eyed her.

Cammy saw what would come next. Lonely days and nights in front of the television. The bit of a beer belly eventually spilling over his belt. Stubble turning into a beard. An oxygen mask that wouldn't seal.

All those nights worrying about him. Never about her mother. Never about herself.

Cammy made the 'A-Ok' sign with her fingers and popped her lips. She studied her father. Locked him into her memory.

Mustache. No beard. Not yet. She turned and watched the exit signs reel by. "Just saying goodbye."

ACKNOWLEDGMENTS

Eternal gratitude to the following literary magazines and journals for publishing pieces appearing in this collection.

"Classified Ad for a Ghost" *Fractured Lit* March '23
"The Swear Jar" *Barren Magazine* Issue 23
"Closer Than Gone" *Sonora Review* April '23
"Shooting at Hurricanes" *Bull* March '24
"Tuesday May Never Come" *Chestnut Review* Winter '23
"Impact" *HAD* August '24

My love and thanks to the Flashpack crew: Dawn Miller, Elissa Fields, Amy Marques, Dawn Steffler, Claudia Monpere, Kim Steutermann Rogers, and Melissa Llanes Brownlee. And my gratitude to Maria S. Picone and the *Chestnut Review* family for believing in this book.

ABOUT THE AUTHOR

Mario Aliberto III's short fiction has appeared in *SmokeLong Quarterly, Fractured Lit, The Pinch, trampset, Tahoma Literary Review, JMWW*, and other fine journals. He is a SmokeLong Quarterly Workshop Prize runner-up, and his work has received nominations for The Pushcart Prize, Best of the Net, Best Small Fictions, and Best Microfiction. A graduate with a Creative Writing degree from the University of South Florida, he lives in Tampa Bay with his wife and daughters, and yet the dog still runs the house. Find him online at marioaliberto3.com.

www.ingramcontent.com/pod-product-compliance
Lightning Source LLC
Chambersburg PA
CBHW031626310726
48974CB00003B/844